RUPERT

RUPERT AND
PONG PING

RUPERT AND
THE BLUE STAR

This edition first published in Great Britain
in 1983 by

Octopus Books Limited
59 Grosvenor Street
London W1

This arrangement © 1983 Octopus Books Limited

From *Rupert and Pong Ping* first published in Great Britain
in 1982 by Express Newspapers Limited © Express
Newspapers Ltd. 1982. Illustrations by Alfred Bestall.
From *Rupert and the Blue Star* first published in Great Britain
in 1975 by Beaverbrook Newspapers Limited © Beaverbrook
Newspapers Ltd., 1975. Illustrations by Alfred Bestall.

ISBN 0 86273 097 X

Produced by
Mandarin Publishers Limited
22a Westlands Road
Quarry Bay, Hong Kong

Printed in Hong Kong

CONTENTS

RUPERT AND PONG PING
4

RUPERT AND THE BLUE STAR
38

RUPERT AND PONG PING

Rupert is strolling through a field near Nutwood one day when he spies his chum Pong Ping, the little Peke, sitting on a fence, looking very glum. As he gets nearer he sees that Pong Ping has been crying, which is not like him.

'I say, what's up?' Rupert asks.

'Oh, I'm so very homesick,' the Peke sniffs.

'But *this* is your home,' says Rupert.

'Not always,' replies Pong Ping. 'Climb up here and I'll explain.'

'I was born in a far-off land where my father was the Emperor's favourite,' Pong Ping begins and at the same time produces a medallion. 'The Emperor gave him this badge and I wear it in memory of him. How I wish I could go back for a visit.'

'It *is* difficult, isn't it,' Rupert murmurs. Then he has an idea.

'Let's ask the Professor!' he exclaims. And a moment later the chums are hurrying towards their old friend's tower house.

'That's Pong Ping sitting over there.
And crying, too!' says Rupert Bear.

'Why, what's the matter?' Rupert cries.
'I'm homesick,' poor Pong Ping replies.

Pong Ping's medallion makes him ache
A journey to his home to take.

'The old Professor's sure to know
Some way or other you may go!'

irst we must find out where your far-off land is,' the Professor says when he hears Pong Ping's problem. 'Your medal may give us a clue.' And he studies the medallion closely then takes down book after book and pores through them.

'Got it!' he cries at last. 'This medal comes from a land deep in the Far, Far East. I can't *send* you there. But perhaps I can get a message through for you.'

Next moment Rupert and Pong Ping find themselves in the Professor's very own radio room. The chums have never seen anything like it, and they gaze, open-mouthed, as the Professor twiddles and tunes and turns knobs and dials. At last he nods and puts on a pair of earphones.

'Nutwood calling!' he repeats into the microphone then listens hard. He frowns and shakes his head. 'I've got through, all right. But I can't understand a word they're saying.'

'Let me try!' Pong Ping cries. 'I speak the language of that country.' And the Peke jumps up and down in excitement.

'This medal's from too far away
For me to send you, I must say.'

'My radio room is close at hand.
We'll try to speak to that far land.'

The old man twirls the knobs around,
And presently they hear a sound.

Alas, the words don't mean a thing.
'I'll understand them,' cries Pong Ping.

At once the Professor gives Pong Ping the earphones and stands him on a chair in front of the microphone. Rupert watches his friend getting more and more excited as by turn he listens and talks in a language that the little bear does not understand. When Pong Ping at last jumps down from the chair he does a little dance of joy.

'I've spoken to the Emperor himself,' he shouts in glee. 'And what do you think? He's going to send for me to go on a visit to him!'

The two chums thank the old Professor for his help and dash excitedly back to Nutwood.

'The Emperor didn't say how he was going to send for me,' pants Pong Ping, 'but for such a long journey it surely must be by airplane!'

Rupert is happy for his pal and he says, 'You go and pack your things and I'll keep watch.'

Rupert hurries home, explains what is happening, begs some sandwiches and lemonade from Mrs Bear then makes his way to a hillside that faces east and starts his lookout.

So Pong Ping stands upon a chair
And listens in with special care.

'The Emperor spoke!' he cries with glee,
'And said, 'Please come and stay with me''.'

They think the Emperor's sure to send
His fastest 'plane to fetch his friend.

So Rupert watches from a crag
While Pong Ping goes to pack his bag.

upert waits and watches all afternoon but there is no sign of any airplane. Next day and the day after that, he and Pong Ping take turns at keeping watch. Then just when Rupert thinks nothing is ever going to appear, the hillside starts to shake.

As rocks begin to fall Rupert jumps up and dashes towards home. To his horror the earth-quake seems to be everywhere and he sees little animals fleeing in terror.

'This is awful,' pants poor Rupert as he runs. 'What can be happening?'

Every second the earthquake gets worse with the ground shaking and trembling. Then the ground just behind Rupert heaves and pitches him on to his face.

Thoroughly frightened, he scrambles behind a rock and looks back. And gasps! For, from a hole in the earth has crawled out the most strange machine. It has great claw wheels and a spinning nose for boring through the earth. Then to his amazement, a door opens and two foreign-looking men climb out.

One day while Rupert's looking out,
The hill begins to shake about.

The trees shake too, the squirrels flee,
And Rupert runs, fast as can be.

And then there bursts with frightful sound,
A metal monster through the ground.

Frightened, poor Rupert runs to hide,
As from the monster two men stride.

oping he has not been spotted, Rupert hides behind a tree. But the two strangers have seen him and run straight to where he is hiding. At once they start to talk very fast. Poor Rupert can't understand a word they say, then all at once he spots that both are wearing round their necks medallions like Pong Ping's.

'Why, of course, you're the Emperor's messengers!' he exclaims happily. Then, making signs that he will return soon, he runs to find Pong Ping.

Rupert doesn't have far to go, for Pong Ping has come out to see what all the noise and shaking is about.

'Quick!' shouts Rupert, 'your friends from the Emperor are here! They didn't come by airplane after all. They were in a sort of tank thing that goes under the ground!'

At first Pong Ping can't understand what Rupert is talking about, but then he spots the strangers and rushes towards them, chattering excitedly.

'Oh, I do wish I knew what they were saying,' thinks Rupert.

Around their necks hang shiny things;
Medallions just like Pong Ping's.

'You're from the Emperor!' Rupert cries.
'I'll fetch Pong Ping', and off he flies.

'Your friends,' shouts Rupert to his chum,
'By some strange kind of tank have come!'

Then off to greet them Pong Ping hies.
'So glad to see you, friends!' he cries.

Pong Ping turns to Rupert.

'You're quite right,' he says. 'They are from the Emperor and they've come to take me to him. But let's have a joyride first, shall we?'

'Rather!' cries Rupert. So they scramble in and shut the door. But at once the machine plunges back into the hole from which it came. Rupert shouts at the driver to turn back but he doesn't understand. Then he turns to Pong Ping who is smiling mischievously.

'I told him to do that,' says the Peke. 'I want you to come with me on holiday! Sorry, Rupert, but I do like to have someone with me and I'm sure you'll like it.'

'Oh, well—,' Rupert agrees. But he still finds the journey through the earth long and dark and he is relieved when they emerge beside a river.

After Pong Ping and the two men have spoken together, the little Peke says, 'They say we must make our own way from here. They've told me what we must do. They say that first we have to make for that bridge over there. So let's go.'

A ride for Rupert is proposed.
They jump in and the door is closed.

The strange machine with mighty roar,
Descends into the earth once more.

At length they reach a distant land
With mountains very steep and grand.

'We leave you now,' the two men say.
'You cross that bridge to find your way.'

The bridge, when they come to it, is very steep and seems to lead nowhere but the steep sides of a high mountain. But Pong Ping doesn't hesitate. He leads the way upward until at last he stops and points to a crevice in the rock. Rupert can just make out a kind of trumpet.

'That's what I was told to look for,' says Pong Ping. 'We have to blow it. Since you're stronger than I am you'd better do the blowing.'

Mystified, Rupert climbs up and takes the strange instrument. He puts the trumpet to his lips and blows. To his delight it makes a loud, beautiful sound. Almost at once, in answer to the call, two great birds appear from beyond the mountain and fly towards the chums.

'Climb on to our backs and hold tight!' they cry as they land. That is a lot easier said than done because their feathers are so smooth, but at length the pals are in position.

'Off we go!' cry the birds, and with that launch themselves into space.

They cross the bridge named by their guide,
And come upon a mountain side.

And there they see, as they were told,
A trumpet that is plainly old.

The trumpet's notes sound loud and clear.
And now two splendid birds appear.

'Come, scramble on our backs,' they cry.
They stretch their wings and off they fly.

High over the mountains fly the great birds with Rupert and Pong Ping clinging to their backs. At first Rupert can hardly bear to open his eyes but when he does so he sees a magnificent city below. Its buildings have spiky roofs and bright-coloured walls.

'The Emperor's secret city,' says the bird as it descends. The two birds put the pals down on a sort of terrace. Just as Rupert is wondering what happens next a fierce-looking soldier appears and says something Rupert doesn't understand.

Pong Ping, though, seems to understand for he produces his medallion and shows it to the soldier. The man studies the medallion and when he hands it back to Ping Pong he is much more respectful. Beckoning the pals to follow, he leads the way to a very large room where a friendly-looking man is seated on a throne.

'The Emperor!' gasps Pong Ping. 'Oh, and that must be his pet dragon.' Just then the Emperor smiles and beckons to them to approach.

They cross a mighty mountain range
To reach a palace rich and strange.

An armoured soldier halts the pair,
And fixes them with frightening stare.

Pong Ping displays his medal rare.
The man at once admits the pair.

Then to the Emperor's room they're shown,
And find him seated on a throne.

My old favourite's son! Welcome, welcome!' cries the Emperor. And Rupert is delighted to hear the kindly ruler speak a language that he understands.

'Well, you must be hungry after your long journey,' the Emperor goes on, and almost at once the friends find themselves at a table with a wonderful meal in front of them. Rupert, though, does have a bit of trouble with his chopsticks at first.

Later when they set out to tour the palace, Rupert, who is lagging behind, hears a hiss from a corner and turns to find the Emperor's pet dragon. To his horror it grabs him by the scruff of the neck and drags him out on to a wide terrace.

'Listen,' it hisses. 'I was the Emperor's favourite till your friend came. Tell him to go back at once or my uncle, the Flying Dragon, will put an end to him—understand?'

He points towards the sky and there Rupert sees the sinister form of the great Flying Dragon.

At supper Rupert's in a fix;
He finds he has to use chopsticks.

A hissing startles Rupert Bear.
He turns. A dragon's lurking there!

The dragon shouts, 'It is a shame!
I've been neglected since you came!'

'My dreaded uncle flying there
Will carry off your friend, young bear.'

o Rupert's astonishment Pong Ping is not at all worried by the dragon's threat.

'I am the Emperor's favourite,' he says. 'No one would dare touch me.'

But Rupert is still uneasy as they settle down to sleep that night. After their long journey the chums are so tired and sleep so soundly that neither sees the frightening figure that glares through their window just as dawn is breaking. It is a cry of fear that wakens Rupert who opens his eyes to see his chum being hauled through the window by a great scaly claw.

'The Flying Dragon!' he cries and, leaping from bed, dashes to the Emperor's chamber to tell him.

But to his dismay the Emperor does nothing but moan, 'Oh, dear, the Flying Dragon! No one can do anything about that, I fear!'

'Oh, please let *me* try to rescue Pong Ping!' cries Rupert.

'Oh, well, if you like,' says the Emperor helplessly. 'I shall send you on a travel-bird after them.' And he has a bird summoned.

That night when both are fast asleep,
The dragon towards them starts to creep.

Rupert is wakened by a squeak.
The dragon's got his pal, the Peke.

Then to the Emperor Rupert goes
And tells of Pong Ping's dragon foes.

'To you a travel-bird I'll lend
To help you find your little friend.'

As Rupert climbs aboard the bird the Emperor says, 'The bird will take you close to the lair of the Flying Dragon. But, oh dear, it is a most dangerous task you have taken on. Good luck!'

The bird heads deep into the mountains where at last it sets Rupert down on a high rock.

'On your own you can never get Pong Ping back,' it says. 'But in that cave down there lives a wise old woman. Ask her advice. If she won't help you then you will never succeed. I shall wait here for you.'

Rupert scrambles down to the cave and just inside it comes upon the wise old woman. She nods as he pours out his story.

'You are a person of great courage, otherwise you would not have got so far,' she says.

Then, handing Rupert a flask, she goes on, 'This is a secret mixture. Somehow you must get the Flying Dragon to drink it. If he does he will sleep for half a day and only then you may be able to rescue your friend. But it will not be easy. Good luck!'

The bird says, 'To a cave we'll go.
A wise old woman's there, I know.'

'And to her words you must give heed.
Without her help you can't succeed.'

The wise old woman hears his tale
And says, 'Your courage must prevail.'

'This drink will make the dragon sleep
For many hours in slumber deep.'

Rupert scrambles back to the bird which carries him the rest of the way to the lair of the Flying Dragon, a deep valley.

'You must go on alone,' it says. 'Each evening two of us birds will return here in case you rescue your friend. Good luck!'

And off it flies. So Rupert makes his way into the valley until a munching noise stops him. He edges forward and, peeping from behind a rock, sees the dragon eating the top branches of a tree.

'How can I get it to drink the sleeping mixture?' Rupert wonders aloud.

'He doesn't drink anything for fear of putting out the fire he breathes,' pipes up a little voice. Rupert turns to see a very small lizard.

'None of us here likes the Flying Dragon,' it goes on. 'So I'll tell you that your only hope is to paint the leaves of one of his food trees with your mixture.'

It points out a good tree and Rupert sets to, using his scarf to paint all its leaves with the sleeping mixture.

The bird takes Rupert all the way,
And says, 'I'll call here every day.'

The dragon's eating from a tree,
But no Pong Ping can Rupert see.

'He never drinks,' a lizard cries.
'You'll have to catch him otherwise.'

'Because the drinking plan's no use,
I'll paint the dragon's tree with juice.'

When he has painted all the leaves Rupert finds a safe spot and settles down for the night.

It is daylight when he wakens and once more he steals down into the valley. To his delight he finds that the Flying Dragon must have returned during the night and eaten up all of the tree.

'After gobbling down all that sleeping mixture it can't have got far,' he thinks and sets out to explore.

And, sure enough, he soon comes across the tail of the dragon. The rest of it is hidden behind a rock. But is it asleep? Holding his breath, he peeps round the rock. Ah! The dragon is fast asleep and gently breathing fire.

'Whew!' Rupert lets out a sigh. Now to find Pong Ping. Keeping as quiet as he can, Rupert hunts among the rocks, but no trace of his pal can he find.

'I'll just have to shout for him and risk wakening the dragon,' he decides.

He climbs on to a rock a little way from the dragon and shouts, 'Pong Ping! It's me—Rupert! Where are you?'

'My trick's worked!' Rupert cries in glee.
'The dragon's eaten all the tree!'

He finds the dragon lying still.
Can he the rescue now fulfil?

Towards the giant beast he creeps
To make quite sure the dragon sleeps.

But when in vain he hunts about,
He says, 'I'll have to risk a shout.'

A slight noise from where the dragon lies asleep makes Rupert start and swing round. To his great relief the beast is still slumbering, and peeping from behind a nearby rock is Pong Ping, still in his pyjamas. In hurried whispers Rupert explains about the sleeping mixture.

'But we must hurry before the mixture stops working!' he declares, and taking Pong Ping by the hand, leads him up the steep side of the valley to where the birds have arranged to come each evening.

As they reach the spot two travel-birds appear and very soon the pals are flying back to the Emperor's palace which they reach as dawn is breaking.

The kindly old ruler is delighted at Pong Ping's rescue and orders that Rupert be awarded a golden medal for his bravery. But the rejoicing does not last long. No sooner is Pong Ping properly dressed again than an aged courtier appears.

'Majesty,' he quavers, 'these two must not stay here. Come, I shall show you the reason why.'

When Rupert turns, his foe still sleeps,
But round a boulder Pong Ping peeps.

He says, to still poor Pong Ping's fright,
'The birds will meet us here tonight.'

'Well done, brave bear!' the Emperor cries.
'My golden medal is your prize.'

But now a courtier cries with fear,
'Oh, sire, these two must not stay here.'

The old courtier leads the way on to the terrace and points at the sky.

'There!' he cries. 'The Flying Dragon! Awake once more and I am quite sure looking for its escaped captive. If he finds Pong Ping here he will breathe fire upon us in his anger and burn us all up!'

'Oh, dear! Gracious me!' gasps the Emperor who, though kind, is not at all brave. 'We'd better get them away.' And at once a guard is summoned and told to take the two chums out of sight.

The burly guard picks up Rupert and Pong Ping and, followed by the Emperor, hurries them deep into the palace cellars. He sets them down on two mats at the edge of a hole in the floor.

'Sorry about this,' the Emperor says. 'Come again when things are a bit quieter.'

'Thank you,' Pong Ping replies. 'I should love it if things really *were* a bit quieter.'

The Emperor nods. The guard gives the chums a push—and then suddenly they are sliding downwards through the earth in pitch darkness.

The courtier points towards the sky,
And there they see the dragon fly.

The chums are hurried out of sight
For fear of that fierce dragon's spite.

The Emperor says, 'I can't, you see,
Keep you two longer here with me.'

So down the cellar chute they slide;
A steep and dark and bumpy ride.

Faster and faster the chums slide down the steep, dark slope. Then suddenly the slope is not so steep, there is daylight ahead and they swish into the open where a smooth rock checks their speed and prevents their being dashed on to the boulders below.

Gazing around, Rupert exclaims, 'I know where we are! This is where we started from before we called the birds.'

And so very carefully the two chums climb down over the boulders to the river. They cross the steep bridge again and start across the plain.

'See! There's the tank thing that brought us here!' Rupert cries. Just then the driver of the tank spies the pals and runs to them. To Rupert's surprise he finds himself grabbed by the man who chatters sternly at them.

'He says we should still be at the palace,' explains Pong Ping. 'He has had no orders about us.' But at that moment Rupert spies one of the Emperor's travel-birds with something in its beak.

When they are nearly in despair
They shoot into the open air.

And Rupert gives a happy shout,
'It was from here we started out!'

They clamber down towards the plain
And see their driver once again.

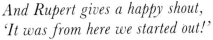

And then a bird towards them flies.
'It brings a message,' Rupert cries.

he great bird lands beside the driver who takes a scroll from its beak, unrolls it and reads.

'That's the Emperor's orders about you,' the bird explains. 'I tried to get here first but you travelled so fast I was left behind.' The driver finishes reading and without a word he lifts the chums and hurries to the tank.

'I think we're going home,' gasps Rupert.

'I hope so!' Pong Ping says. 'I shall never be homesick for this part of the world again.'

Some time later, back in Nutwood, Rupert's Mummy and Daddy, who are on their way to ask the police if anything has been seen of Rupert, suddenly hear a rumbling and find themselves face to face with a strange machine.

In another moment Rupert and Pong Ping have jumped out, the machine has bored its way back into the earth and Mr and Mrs Bear are peering, amazed, down the hole that goes to the Far, Far East.

'I'll tell you all about it over supper!' laughs Rupert.

'The Emperor's orders,' says the bird.
The driver reads the royal word.

Then in his arms the chums he takes
And for the tank he quickly makes.

Loud rumbling gives the Bears a fright,
And then the tank comes into sight.

'You see this hole?' says Rupert Bear.
'We've been to Pong Ping's land down there.'

RUPERT AND THE BLUE STAR

Mr Bear is taking the family and Rupert's pal Bill Badger for a day at the sea. As Rupert and Bill are carrying the picnic things to the car, the familiar figure of Sailor Sam comes striding down the hill.

'Hello, Sam,' says Rupert. 'We're off to the seaside.'

'How I envy you!' says Sam. 'I haven't been to the sea for ages.'

'Cheer up! We'll bring you a present,' smiles Rupert. When he asks the sailor what he would like, Sam grins.

'Just bring anything to remind me of my days at sea.' He waves goodbye and off goes the car. After a long journey they spy the sea and stop on a grassy verge. Bill jumps out and runs towards the cliffs.

'We'll choose a picnic spot,' says Mrs Bear, 'while you go exploring.'

'Don't go far,' says Mr Bear. 'We can't stay long.'

'Hi, Sailor Sam! We're just away,
Off to the seaside for the day.'

'We'll bring a present back for you,'
Smiles Rupert, 'as you can't come too.'

Sam waves goodbye. 'That would be kind,
No sharks or whales or swordfish, mind!'

'We'll have our picnic on the shore,'
Says Mummy. 'Then you can explore.'

The little party has its picnic near the sea and then Rupert and Bill climb to the top of the cliffs.

'Hi, look there,' cries Bill. 'D'you see those masts appearing over the edge? There must be a ship in that cove. I wish we could reach it.'

'I'm afraid we can't,' says Rupert. 'We promised not to go far, but I do wish I knew what ship it is.' They decide to go down towards the sea by a rough gully and find it very steep. All at once Rupert notices a wide crack in the side of the gully.

'I don't believe we can get down the rocks to the shore,' he says. 'This dark hole looks exciting. Shall we see where it leads?' Bill is always keen for something new and soon the two pals have squeezed into a gloomy cave below.

'There's light beyond,' says Bill. 'There must be another way out.'

'Hey, what's this on the floor?' says Rupert. 'It's a little sack. And look what's fallen out of it. Surely it's a starfish. But what a funny colour for a starfish. It's *blue*!'

Along the cliffs the two pals rove,
'Look! There's a ship moored in that cove!'

They clamber down. 'This gully's steep!
And here's a cave! Bill, come and peep!'

Each scrambles through the narrow space,
Says Bill, 'What an exciting place!'

'A starfish, Bill—a blue one, see!
Now that is something new to me!'

Rupert stares at the curious thing on the rough floor.

'*Is* it a starfish?' he says. 'I've never heard of a *blue* one.' He bends down, but before he can touch it there is a hiss from Bill.

'Be quiet! There's someone coming!' he whispers urgently. Sure enough, there are gruff voices and the noise of footsteps crunching on pebbles.

'I don't like the sound of those men,' breathes Rupert. 'Let's be off.' And, as quietly as they can, they climb back towards the gap in the cliff. Out in the open air the two friends retrieve their spades and pails.

'We'll never reach the shore down that steep gully,' says Rupert. 'Let's go up again and return the way we came over the cliff-top.' Once they are on the grass Bill looks wistfully towards the three masts.

'I wish we could see it nearer,' he murmurs. 'I love ships.'

'Come on,' urges Rupert. 'It may belong to those men whose voices we didn't like. Besides, Daddy doesn't want us to be away too long.'

Then crunching footsteps make them shrink!
Breathes Bill, 'They're coming here, I think!'

They hear gruff voices and a cough,
'Quick,' whispers Rupert, 'let's be off!'

'Those men sound rough, we mustn't stop!'
Let's make our way up to the top.'

'I'm glad we gave those men the slip,
Perhaps they came here on that ship.'

When they are halfway back the two pals pause again.

'That way down looks much easier than the gully,' says Rupert. 'The tide's going out, so we should be able to work round the headland and join Mummy and Daddy at their picnic point.

This time they succeed, and make their different way among the rocks and pools of the upper shore.

All at once Rupert, who has been faster than Bill, stares at something as if he can hardly believe what he sees lying on the sand among the rocks. What has startled Rupert is a small object lying between some boulders, an object with five points.

'It's another starfish. Another *blue* one!' he mutters. Going to it he bends down to pick it up. Then he topples back in fright for barely has he touched it when the points curl up and a violent shock runs up his arm. Lifting himself up, he gives a shout just as his pal comes to join him.

'Whatever's up now?' Bill demands. 'Have you had a tumble or lost something? What are you staring at?'

The pals run on, until they reach
An easy pathway to the beach.

A starfish glistens in the sun,
'It's blue! Just like that other one!'

The thing glows with a bluish light,
One touch, and Rupert jumps in fright!

A violent shock runs up his arm,
He cringes back in great alarm.

Moving forward Bill Badger notices the strange thing lying on the shingle.

'What, another *blue* starfish!' he exclaims. 'Where do they come from? Is it alive?'

'Yes, yes it is,' cries Rupert. 'Let it alone. It's dangerous!' But Bill has already touched it, and he leaps back with a scared look as the starfish does its trick again.

'W-what is it?' he say, shakily. 'Is it a real one?' When the two pals feel better after their shocks they stand and gaze at the blue starfish.

'I don't understand how it got here,' says Bill, as an idea strikes him. 'It's still alive, but the sea didn't bring it here. The tide's just going out and didn't come up quite as high as this.'

'I wonder if it was dropped from that sack we saw in the cave,' says Rupert. 'I tell you what—it's just the sort of thing that would interest Sailor Sam. Let's take it back.' And very gingerly he carries his pail nearer and picks up the strange blue starfish on his wooden spade.

'It's still alive, Bill, leave it be!
It's full of electricity!'

Too late! Bill leaps back, 'Oh, my hat!
It's foreign! Ours don't shock like that!'

'It's high and dry!' They stare in awe,
'Perhaps it's from that sack we saw.'

The chums recover in a while,
Says Rupert, 'This will make Sam smile!'

he starfish lies quietly in the pail, and Rupert starts to carry it away.

'It's making my arm feel funny,' he grins. 'That thing must still be alive!'

'Perhaps the poor thing wants some salt water,' says Bill. So they stop at the nearest pool and Bill uses the other bucket to pour in water.

'Now it'll be heavier,' says Rupert. 'I'll carry it first and—Oo!—Ow!—Eee!—I *c-c-can't!* The whole bucket's electric now. I'm tingling all over!' And, in alarm, he drops both his spade and bucket hurriedly.

Meanwhile, Mrs Bear is packing up the picnic things.

'Rupert and Bill have been away a long time,' she says. 'I hope they are safe.'

'See, here they come,' says Mr Bear. 'They're carrying something.'

'Look, Daddy, a new starfish,' says Rupert when he arrives. 'It's blue, and it made the pail too electric to hold, but we found that when we put the wooden spades through the handle we could carry it.'

Mr Bear stares and murmurs: 'My, the things you do find.'

They fill the bucket from a pool,
'It wants salt water, nice and cool.'

'Oo!-Ow! The pail's electric now!
I cannot hold it anyhow!'

With wooden spades to guard their hands,
They bring the pail across the sands.

'Blue starfish? Gives electric shocks?'
Gasps Daddy. 'Stranded near the rocks?'

Mr and Mrs Bear tell the little pals to leave the blue starfish as it is time to go home.

'Oh, *please*, can't we take it with us?' pleads Rupert. 'We promised Sailor Sam that we'd bring him something, and we've seen nothing as interesting as this!' So Mr Bear gives them a large handkerchief to tie over the pail. They all get in, and he tries to start the engine.

'Here, what on earth's happening?' he gasps. For the whole car is now quivering and tingling. So is everyone in it! The engine splutters and wheezes, but will not start, so they all get out.

'The thing you put in there must be causing the trouble,' says Mr Bear. 'It must go or we shall never get home.'

'The pail is as hard to catch hold of as it was before,' says Rupert, as he touches it. 'Let's put the wooden spade through the handle again.' They do so and are soon able to return to the shore.

'I wish I knew how this thing managed to be such a nuisance,' says Bill with a frown.

'We'll take the starfish back for Sam,'
Says Rupert. 'Mind the doors don't slam!'

'The engine won't start! Get outside!
The whole car's gone electrified!'

'It's that blue starfish, I'm afraid,
Remove it! Use a wooden spade!'

'Let's find a pool where it can live!
Poor Sam, we've nothing else to give!'

wish things hadn't turned out quite like this,' murmurs Rupert. 'I did want to take something interesting back to Sailor Sam, and this blue starfish is the oddest thing we've seen today. I expect it needs salt water to keep it alive. Look, here's a pool left at the very top of the tide.'

They put the pail at the edge of the pool, and Rupert gently tips the creature out. Soon they are in the car again.

'Good, there's nothing wrong with the engine now,' says Mr Bear as he drives briskly away. So much time has been wasted because of the unexpected behaviour of the starfish that evening has nearly closed in before Mr Bear brings the hired car safely home.

'Join me again tomorrow, Bill,' says Rupert. 'You must help me tell Sailor Sam all about what we saw at the seaside.'

'Right-o, I'll come,' says Bill. 'I must hurry now, my Daddy will think I'm lost.' And next morning Rupert looks out for him eagerly. When Bill does not appear he becomes impatient.

They tip it in. 'I only wish
Sam could have seen you, Blue Starfish!'

Soon they are in the car again,
And speeding homeward, right as rain.

'Let's call on Sam tomorrow, Bill!
Our tale should give him quite a thrill.'

Next morning Rupert waits alone,
'Bill's late! I'll set off on my own.'

Bill does not turn up at the expected time and Rupert asks Mrs Bear if he may go alone to see his friend Sailor Sam.

'When Bill comes, please tell him that I'm ahead of him,' he says as he sets off. Sailor Sam is in the garden of his shack when he arrives.

'Well, little bear, did you have a good day at the sea?' smiles the sailor. 'Did you bring me a present?'

'Not quite,' laughs Rupert. 'But you'd be surprised at what we nearly brought!' And he tells his friend of all that happened when the blue starfish was put in the car. Sailor Sam walks towards his shack while Rupert is talking.

'I expect you'd like some lemonade and a biscuit,' he smiles. 'What a nice day you had. So you saw the masts of a sailing ship and then found a starfish . . .' He pauses suddenly and swings round.

'What did you say? A blue one?' Going inside he sits down abruptly and stares at the little bear.

'It can't be, it can't be true!' he breathes. 'The *Blue Star*? Are you sure?'

He dashes off without his chum,
'Ahoy!' calls Sam. 'I'm glad you've come.'

Laughs Rupert, 'Sam, we nearly brought
A strange blue starfish that we caught!'

'You saw some ship's masts? Then you found
A blue star . . . What?' Sam whirls around.

'The Blue Star? Are you sure of this?
Then something's very much amiss!'

Rupert is astonished at his friend's excitement.

'Is the blue starfish very rare?' he asks.

'*Rare!* Of course it's rare!' exclaims Sam. 'It only lives in one place in the world.' He unrolls the map of an island.

'There, that's one of Cap'n Morgan's smuggling haunts,' he says. 'It's far, far away and the Blue Star lives there. It could never have travelled all this way alone over the bed of the sea. That means that somebody has troubled to bring Blue Stars here.' Rupert tries hard to understand.

'But why shouldn't people bring them?' he asks.

'Because they're terrible, dangerous, and poisonous,' says Sam. 'You're lucky you only got an electric shock. If you had a scratch from one of its thousands of little spikes you might have been very ill. Now who can have brought that sack full of them?' All of a sudden he gives a gasp.

''Tis Black Pedro!' he shouts. 'It can be no other! Wait, I'll show you.' And he produces a little iron box from its hiding place.

'It comes,' cries Sam, a map unfurled,
'From just one island in the world!'

'It didn't swim this far, or fly!
So someone shipped it here! But why?'

'Black Pedro brought them! Now I guess,
To put me out of action, yes!'

'He wants this box! Aye, that's his plan!
'Twas left me by a sailor man.'

Rupert is now quite bewildered.

'Black Pedro? Who is Black Pedro?' he asks.

'He's my only real enemy,' says Sailor Sam gloomily. 'He knows Cap'n Morgan's island where the Blue Stars can be found. And I believe that he has found out that I've got this. Look.' And from the heavy little box he produces a piece of old, tough brown paper.

'There's writing on it,' says Rupert, 'But I don't understand a word of it.'

'No wonder,' says Sam. 'Neither can I! I don't know that lingo.' Sam ponders over the faded paper.

'The box was left me by an old sailor man who used to be a smuggler himself,' he says. 'This paper was the only thing in it and it's my belief that it tells the secret of a great hidden treasure. If so, it's very, very precious and must be guarded until some clever person tells me its meaning.'

Then Rupert hears a little sound and he goes to the door. Outside there is no one in sight, but lying close to the doorstep is a small package with a label tied to it.

Upon a paper, old and brown,
Some foreign words are written down.

'Its meaning, some wise man must tell,
Till then,' says Sam, 'I'll guard it well.'

'Tis my belief, it tells,' he sighs,
'Where some great hidden treasure lies.'

A rustle's heard outside the door,
'Why, here's a parcel! Who's it for?'

ailor Sam has followed Rupert to the door.
'Look here,' says the little bear. 'This parcel is addressed to you. It wasn't there when we came in. Perhaps it is meant as a surprise. Is it your birthday?'

'No, it isn't! And I don't like people leaving parcels and then sneaking away,' says Sam, who is already in a very nervous state. 'Let me have it.'

He takes it gingerly and unfastens the paper with the greatest care. Then he flicks off the lid. Inside the box is tissue paper and, instead of undoing it, Sam tips it out on the table. Immediately he waves Rupert back.

'Don't touch!' he shouts. 'Look what it is! A Blue Star. It's a dead one, but just as dangerous! Just what I thought, this must be from Black Pedro, who wants me out of action. I must have help. Who can I get? Constable Growler is the nearest. Oh dear, I must go.'

He is so agitated that he dashes straight out, forgetting that he has left Rupert alone at the shack.

'For you, Sam! There's a label on,
Whoever left it here has gone.'

Suspiciously, Sam opens it,
'I'll tip it out, stand back a bit.'

'Don't touch! A Blue Star! Keep your head,
It's dangerous, although it's dead!'

'It's from Black Pedro! I must act!
He means to harm me, it's a fact!'

Things have been happening too fast for poor Rupert since arriving at Sailor Sam's shack, and the sudden departure of his friend leaves him stranded and rather frightened.

'What had I better do?' he thinks, as he goes into the shack again. 'I mustn't touch that awful blue starfish. And, oh goodness me! Sam's forgotten to put away that precious old paper. Suppose anyone comes. That's the one thing he will be anxious not to lose. The best thing I can do, I suppose, is to see to it for him.' Rupert looks at the little iron box.

'I wonder if I can find the place where he hides that,' he murmurs, 'and whether it is too heavy for me to carry.' He tugs it off the table, but just as he gets it into his arms the lid closes with a snap.

'Oh dear, I must open it to put the old paper in,' he thinks. 'I didn't know the lid was on a spring. And now it won't open again! And Sam's taken the key.' All at once he stops to listen.

'What was that noise?' he whispers.

'The Constable's the one I need!'
Sam rushes off at frantic speed.

'Sam's paper! I must put it back!'
Thinks Rupert, trembling, in the shack.

He lifts the box, a heavy thing,
Then – snap! – the lid shuts, on a spring.

'Sam took the key! The lid's tight shut!
What's that? Who's coming to the hut?'

The noise that Rupert has heard comes nearer.

'There's somebody outside,' he thinks. 'That is not Sam's footstep. Who can it be?'

Though he pulls feverishly at the lid of the iron box it will not open. At last he grabs the precious old paper and stuffs it under his jersey. He is just in time to straighten up as the door bursts open and a grim figure in strange clothes strides in.

'And who are you?' growls the man. 'I thought the sailor lived alone.' Rupert is startled and scared by the stranger's sudden appearance.

'Oh p-please, I'm a friend of Sam's,' he quavers. 'And I called to see him because he asked for something from the seaside and . . .' But the other does not seem to be listening. Still frowning he peers keenly around. He looks without surprise at the dead starfish, then rushes towards the iron box.

'That's it, that's it!' he hisses. ''Tis the very thing I came for! Cap'n Morgan's carpenter, Old Jem, owned that box. Many's the time I've seen it. Now 'tis mine!'

Thinks Rupert, 'Good, my jersey's tight,'
He stuffs the paper out of sight.

He's just in time! The door bursts wide,
A grim-faced stranger steps inside.

He sweeps aside the little bear,
Then spies the box, still lying there.

'That's it! The smuggler's box!' he grins.
'And now 'tis mine! The best man wins!'

s the man seizes the black box and tucks it under his arm Rupert screws up his courage to speak.

'Put that down!' he says, trembling. 'It belongs to Sailor Sam, and he's gone to fetch Constable Growler. He'll be back any minute.'

'Oh, will he?' The man seems amused at something. 'I think not, little bear. Black Pedro cannot be caught by simple sailors or country coppers! Nor will he leave *you* here to give the alarm. You come with me.'

And grabbing Rupert, he marches him rapidly out of the shack. The man, holding Rupert firmly, urges him into the nearby woods. The little bear is very scared at what he has heard.

'He spoke of Black Pedro,' he thinks. 'Can he himself be Black Pedro? That's the name of Sailor Sam's enemy. Oh, I do hope that Sam will hurry up and bring help.'

On they go until they reach a rough shelter of branches covered with foliage. Then a fierce-looking man appears and, pointing at the shelter, he says some foreign words.

'That box is Sam's! You leave it here!
He'll bring the policeman, never fear!'

'Black Pedro can't be caught by such!
You come with me! You talk too much.'

'Black Pedro!' Rupert thinks, in dread,
As through deep woodland he is sped.

A hard man, waiting in the glade,
Points at a shelter, roughly made.

he newcomer catches sight of the black box under Pedro's arm and becomes suddenly excited. Pedro grins darkly.

'Yes, it's the very box,' he says. 'The key was not in it but no matter. Search him quickly and get it.' The other man dives into the shelter and Rupert hears noises inside.

'What does it mean?' he thinks. 'Who is being searched?'

In a few minutes the man appears again, looking angry.

'No good, no key, no not'ing,' he whines. 'Him pockets empty.' Black Pedro is very annoyed at what his man has said.

'We must not wait for more,' he growls. 'A cold chisel must serve our purpose as there is no key. Now to get away. But we must not leave that little creature to tell his story until we are well clear. Truss him up and put him out of sight.'

And while the other men gather round, Rupert finds his wrists and ankles tied and his arms bound tightly. Then he is lifted and carried into the semi-darkness of the shelter and dumped on his back.

'Yes, it's the very box, at last!
We need the key, so search him fast!'

The man comes back. 'No key!' he moans.
'Now how we open box?' he groans.

'We'll break it open later on,
Now tie him up, and let's be gone!'

Into the shelter Rupert's borne,
And left there, frightened and forlorn.

Rupert listens to the gruff voices of Black Pedro and his crew, first arguing and then becoming fainter, and by squirming over he manages to sit up in time to see the men disappearing downhill. While he is wondering what he can do to get free from the ropes he hears another sound, muffled and much nearer.

'There's somebody else here,' he breathes. After more squirming he is able to kneel up and peer into the darkness of the shelter.

'Surely I can see a pair of boots!' he whispers. 'There *is* someone here!'

Knowing that he is not alone, Rupert calls into the darkness. The answer is a low grunt and a straining noise. Rupert contrives to shuffle forward and to his astonishment, he makes out the figure of his friend Sailor Sam lying bound in the darkness with a cloth tied over his mouth.

'Oh Sam, what have they done to you? How did they catch you?' he gasps. Suddenly he turns.

'Listen!' he whispers urgently. 'There, *another* voice. Somebody's calling my name!'

The men run off and disappear,
Then he hears muffled sounds, quite near.

He shuffles forward on his knees,
'A pair of boots! Who is it, please?'

'Oh Sam, what have they done to you?'
Gasps Rupert. 'Now what shall we do?'

He turns abruptly, on his guard,
'Who called my name?' he listens hard.

Rupert shouts in answer to the call and tries to shuffle back. Before he can reach the entrance a familiar figure hurries forward.

'Oh Bill, Bill, I am glad to see you!' cries the little bear. 'Where have you been?'

'I had to run errands for my Mummy, so I couldn't join you when you went to see Sam,' says Bill, 'but I went later and saw you dragged away and I've followed, keeping out of sight. What does it all mean?'

He rapidly unfastens Rupert's cords and listens to the strange story. When Rupert is free, he and Bill lose no time in undoing the cords on Sailor Sam's ankles and arms.

'Those villains were waiting in ambush as I ran for Constable Growler,' says Sam angrily. 'They overpowered me, but why were *you* caught, little bear?'

'Your enemy Black Pedro came to your shack,' says Rupert. 'He stole your heavy little black box and then he dragged me here in case I told anyone. Wasn't it wonderful luck that my pal Bill saw what happened?'

'Why, Bill, it's you! How glad I am!
Quick, rescue me and Sailor Sam!'

'I saw you dragged away, and then
I followed, hiding in the glen.'

Frowns Sam, 'They trapped me as I left,
Then dumped me in this leafy cleft.'

'Black Pedro came, your enemy!
He stole your black box! Where's the key?'

Sailor Sam stands up and looks quite baffled.

'Those rogues are too clever,' he moans.

'But they did fail when they searched me for the key of the box. At the moment I was grabbed I managed to drop the key into the long grass without their seeing it, so that they should not get it. And what can we do now?' Rupert hesitates, but Bill speaks up.

'I've been hiding and have watched what happened,' he says. 'Those men have gone towards the river.'

'Then let's keep them in sight,' says Sam grimly. Going cautiously and listening to every sound, Sam leads the little pals downhill, and at length they reach the river.

'Too late!' growls the sailor. 'What terrible luck. They've got too much start of us. Oh, the rascals! They'll go back to their ship.'

'Can't we still tell Constable Growler?' asks Rupert nervously.

'He might be able to alert the coastguards,' says Sam. 'It's our only chance.' And, puffing with his efforts, he trots uphill again ahead of his chums.

Sighs Sam, 'I dropped it on the way,
But he will force the lock, I'd say.'

'They took the river path,' says Bill.
'Let's follow! We may catch them still.'

'Those rogues have given us the slip,'
Says Sam. 'They're making for their ship!'

'The coastguards! They're the men to get!'
And Sam trots off, not beaten yet.

Near the top of the slope sailor Sam sinks on to a boulder and mops his brow.

"'Tis no use,' he gasps breathlessly. 'Can't keep up this sort of thing—too old for hurrying uphill—never could run much, anyway—oh, dear, oh, dear—iron box gone—Black Pedro gone, never catch him now—oh, dear.' Suddenly Rupert gives a start.

'No, no, you're wrong!' he shouts. 'All this excitement made me forget what happened. Black Pedro has gone, and he has the iron box, but he *hasn't* got the old paper!' Sailor Sam stares at the little bear.

'What d'you mean?' he demands. 'How do you know? If Black Pedro hasn't got the ancient paper, where is it?'

'It's here!' laughs Rupert. 'I've got it myself! When I first heard Pedro coming I was scared. I didn't know where to hide the paper, so I stuffed it in the only place I could think of. See, here it is!'

And from under his jersey he pulls the precious, faded sheet. Sam seizes it, and for some moments he cannot say a word.

But now his head begins to spin,
'Can't keep this up! I'm all done in!'

'They haven't won! That's where you're wrong!
The paper's been safe, all along!'

'I quite forgot in all this haste!'
And Rupert pulls it from his waist.

Sam seizes it in disbelief,
Then gazes, speechless with relief.

When Sailor Sam realizes that his main anxiety has so suddenly been removed he forgets how tired he is, and, waving the paper in the air, he dances a little hornpipe in his delight.

'So it's not lost. It's not lost!' he laughs as he capers about. 'This may make my fortune yet. Just think what we've done to Black Pedro. He's got the iron box without the key. How lovely! I'd give a lot to see his face when he chisels it open and finds it empty! Come on, Rupert! That was smart work!'

Sailor Sam, now feeling as spry as ever, takes the little pals back to his shack.

'That Blue Star is still on the table,' he says. 'It's dead, but it's as poisonous and dangerous as ever.' Picking it up between two pieces of wood he carries it out to bury it.

'And is that the end of the adventure?' asks Rupert.

'Well, it's time you went home,' says Sam, 'but it's not the end by any means. I'll call for you tomorrow.'

'That sounds very mysterious,' Rupert smiles as they scamper off.

Dancing a hornpipe in his joy,
He laughs, 'My paper's safe! Ahoy!'

'I'd love to see Black Pedro's scowl!
That empty box will make him growl!'

'I've buried that dead starfish, true!
But we have one more job to do.'

The chums race home across the green,
'Another task? What does Sam mean?'

Still wondering about Sailor Sam's latest words the two pals reach the Bears' cottage.

'Oo, Mummy, we've had such a time!' says Rupert. 'If it wasn't for Bill I shouldn't be here now. He's got to go to his home, but he'll be back tomorrow and Sailor Sam wants us both and . . .'

'Here, here, not so fast,' says Mrs Bear. 'You're very late. Come in and have your tea.' And she listens to the strange story.

Next morning, after breakfast, Rupert looks out.

'Sam's here, just as he said he would be,' he calls. Rupert finds Sailor Sam holding a mysterious contraption and securing all sorts of things to his old motor-bike and sidecar.

'I picked up Bill to save time,' says Sam. Just then Mrs Bear bustles towards them.

'What's all this?' she demands. 'This affair with dangerous starfishes frightens me. Can't you leave Rupert alone now?'

'No, Ma'am,' says the sailor firmly. 'It's because they're dangerous that I *do* need Rupert now. But I'll keep him quite safe.'

'Oh Mummy, there's so much to tell!
Sam wants us both again, as well!'

Next morning Rupert gives a shout,
'Sam's here, with Bill!' He dashes out.

'Hello,' grins Sam, 'I thought you'd like
A trip on my old motor-bike.'

'Could they ride in my sidecar please?'
He asks, and Mrs Bear agrees.

Having persuaded Mrs Bear to give her consent, Sailor Sam puts Rupert and Bill into his sidecar and the old motor-bike roars away.

'This isn't very comfortable,' says Bill as they bounce along. 'What are we sitting on?'

'Probably my gumboots,' shouts Sam above the din.

'What a weird lot of stuff you're carrying,' shouts Rupert.

'Never mind about that,' says Sam. 'All I want you to do is to guide me to the spot where you left the live Blue Star.' Rupert does so and they all descend to the rocks.

Picking out their landmarks, Rupert and Bill find the spot where they put the starfish into the water. There is no sign of it now, but they call to Sailor Sam who hurries to them wearing his gum-boots and carrying a wooden pail, wooden-handled spade and his curious object with lots of hosepipe.

'I expect you see my idea,' he says. 'You told me that you had left that Blue Star in the very highest pool left by the tide. The odds are that it's still there!'

They set off, with a heavy load,
And drive along the coastal road.

Says Sam, 'You came here? Right you are!
Now, guide me to that live Blue Star!'

'Yes, here's the pool! We've found the spot!
But is the Star still there, or not?'

Sam follows with a load of gear,
'One little test will make that clear.'

Rupert and Bill show Sam the exact spot where the starfish was tipped into the water, and the sailor dips his finger gingerly. Then he rises in great excitement.

'The water's electric. The Star's still there!' he exclaims. Walking into the pool he stands his strange instrument in front of him.

'This is what they call a stirrup pump,' he says. 'Your daddy will know what it's for. Will you take this hose and carry the end a little way off? It's rubber and won't make your fingers tingle.' Rupert takes the end of the hosepipe away from the pool and beyond a boulder.

'Point the nozzle well away from you,' says Sailor Sam, 'And don't get splashed with this electrified water. There's no wind, so it won't be blown back on to you.' Then he works the pump vigorously and a jet of water appears.

At length there is a cry from Sam and, dropping the hose, the two pals find him lifting the Blue Star from the nearly-empty pool, and putting it into the wooden bucket.

'Yes, yes! The pool's electric! Fine!
Let's use that stirrup pump of mine!'

'You take this hosepipe,' Rupert's told,
'I's rubber, and quite safe to hold.'

Sam works the pump with all his strength,
'Right, that's enough!' he calls, at length.

'The live Blue Star! We'll take it home,
It's dangerous, and mustn't roam.'

Rupert is delighted at the success of their work.

'The Blue Star was there safe enough, hiding under a bit of seaweed,' he grins.

'I'll warrant it's the first one ever to be found alive in these parts,' says Sailor Sam. He puts water in the pail and carries it to a safe place up on the cliff-top.

'Now you must show me where your cave with the little sack of dead starfishes was,' he says, and Rupert and Bill lead the way.

'Those masts that we saw here yesterday have disappeared,' says Bill. 'They *must* have belonged to Black Pedro's ship!' Rupert and Bill show Sailor Sam the crack by which they reached the cave.

'I'm a bit too big to get in there,' murmurs Sam. However, he does manage it and takes a coil of rope with him. Later, he appears again.

'The sack of Blue Stars was still there,' he says. 'I'll bury them at once, so there'll be no danger of them hurting other folk. Here they are, tied with my cord.' He drops the sack and sets to work digging near some bushes.

'Now where's that sack of which you spoke?'
Those dead Stars could cause harm to folk.'

Back to the motor-bike they climb,
Says Sam, 'We'll need a rope this time.'

They find the gully, cave and all,
Sam squeezes in, then gives a call.

The sack of dead Blue Stars is found,
Then safely buried in the ground.

Well, we really are getting on,' grins Sam, as he ties a cloth over his bucket. 'Now that electrified water can't splash you. We'll pack up and go. The dangerous part of the affair is over. Now for the interesting bit.'

'I wonder what he means,' says Bill. On the return journey the sailor stops short of Nutwood and they all trot across a slope.

'Why, that's the old Professor's house,' says Rupert. 'Is that where we're going?' Sailor Sam sends Rupert on ahead to see if anyone is at home, and almost at once the small figure of the Professor's servant appears in sight.

'Hello, have you come to see my master?' says the kindly dwarf. 'I'll call him.' Soon they are all at the front door, and the Professor is welcoming them.

'Come in, come in,' he says genially. 'I like Rupert to call. He always brings something interesting.'

'Well, it's not me this time,' Rupert smiles. 'It's Sailor Sam who has brought something interesting. It's in this bucket. May we show you?'

'They're harmless now, and no mistake,
Let's go! We've one more call to make.'

At length they stop, and cross a slope,
'The old Professor's in, I hope.'

The servant looks up from his tasks,
'Rupert! What brings you here?' he asks.

'Professor!' cries the little bear,
'Sam's brought you something very rare!'

After peering into the wooden bucket the old Professor becomes very eager and, fetching a transparent plastic bowl, he helps Sam to tip the Blue Star into it.

'Isn't it a horrid, poisonous thing?' says Rupert. But the old gentleman is gazing in delight.

'This is going to be the pride of my collection,' he gloats. 'It shall have a tank to itself. Never did I expect to have anything so rare!'

While he moves to make arrangements Sam quietly pulls something from the top of his jacket. It is the precious faded paper that was the cause of the whole adventure, and now he tells the Professor of the escape they have had.

'H'm, it must be more than usually important,' says the old gentleman. 'Let's see, what's it written in? It's no language that I know. I do believe that it's old Sea-dog Spanish. We must look into this.'

Going into his library he takes down a small volume and studies the wording on the faded paper carefully. Gradually his face shows a satisfied smile.

'The Blue Star, Rupert! What a find!
I'll keep it, yes. You're very kind.'

'The Star has found a safe retreat!'
Then Sam reveals the precious sheet.

Now, telling all that has occurred,
Sam sighs, 'I can't translate one word.'

'It's Sea-dog Spanish! We must look
In this old Spanish language book.'

he old Professor checks and re-checks the words on the precious paper. Then he points to an island on one of the maps.

'It's quite clear now,' he says. 'That paper tells of great treasure buried by a former pirate on the south-west coast of this island.'

'Well, of all things!' Sam laughs. ''Tis the very island where Black Pedro and his gang have their lair! They may be walking over the treasure every day and never knowing it!'

The Professor is nearly as excited as Sailor Sam.

'My, my, I wish I was young enough to be with you when you sail away to find that treasure,' he says, as the three visitors set out for home. Outside his own cottage Rupert turns eagerly.

'Please, please will you take me with you when you go treasure-hunting?' he pleads. 'Surely *I'm* young enough.' Sailor Sam smiles happily.

'We'll see when the time comes,' he says. 'I can't make promises yet, not while your Mummy is giving me one of her old-fashioned looks!'

'It tells where buried treasure lies,
On this far isle!' the old man cries.

'To think Black Pedro doesn't know!
That island is his lair! Ho-ho!'

The old man calls, 'I wish you luck!
You'll find that treasure, you've got pluck!'

Pleads Rupert Bear, 'You mustn't fail
To take me with you, when you sail!'

AN ISLAND PUZZLE FOR RUPERT

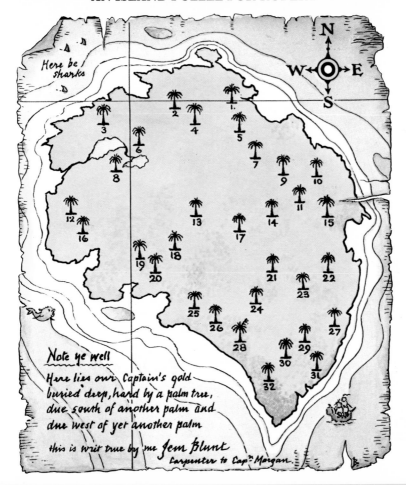

When Sam finds a precious paper that used to belong to old Jem the carpenter, he gets very excited. 'Look at this, Rupert!' he cries. 'Here's a map of a sandy island that grows nothing but palm trees, and they all have numbers. Now we can go straight to where the treasure is buried!'

Why is Sam so sure? First read the story of the Blue Star, then follow the clues written on this map and see if you can spot the palm tree beside which the pirate captain's gold is buried. The answer to the puzzle is on page 96.

AN ISLAND PUZZLE FOR RUPERT
page 95

Three palm trees, Nos. 13, 21 and 28, each stand due south of another palm and due west of yet another, but on the last page of the Blue Star story the old Professor says the treasure is buried on the south-west coast of the island, so palm No. 28 must be the answer.